Celestino Piatti

W9-CPC-372

The Happy Owls

AN ALADDIN BOOK
Atheneum

J
P. C

OCT '80

The Happy Owls
a legend illustrated by Celestino Piatti

Once upon a time
in an old stone ruin
there lived a pair of owls.

All the year through
they were very happy.

On a farm nearby
there were all kinds of barnyard fowl
who did nothing all day
but eat and drink.

And after they had finished eating
and drinking, they began to fight
with one another.

They could never think of
anything better to do.

One day the peacock noticed the owls
and he wanted to know
why they did not quarrel.

Why was it they were so happy?

The other birds
when they heard his question said,
"Why don't you visit the owls
and ask them how they can live together
so peacefully?"

With a deep bow the peacock agreed
to call on the owls.

The peacock carefully preened
his gorgeous plumage
and strutted off in all his finery.

At the owls' house,
he spread out his tail feathers
and rustled them and clawed at the ground
to attract the owls' attention.

The owls blinked their big round eyes
when they heard what he wanted to know.

"Well, Mr. Peacock, we'll tell you,
but first go and fetch all your friends."

When the chickens, the ducks,
the geese and all the others
were assembled,
the owls began their story.

"When spring comes we are happy
to see everything come to life
after the long winter sleep.

The trees put forth their buds and leaves;
the meadows are covered
with thousands of tiny flowers;
and birds everywhere are singing merrily.

Later, around every flower,
bees and bumblebees are buzzing,
and all kinds of little flies are humming.

Butterflies flit to and fro gathering honey
from the golden sunflowers.

Then we know that summer is here.

And when everything is green and growing,
and the trees nod their leafy crowns to us
in the warm sunshine,
we sit in a shady nook in the cool forest
and are at peace with the world.

Then autumn comes,
and the spider, who has waited
through the glorious summer under a leaf,
comes out and spins her web
to hold up the tired leaves a little longer.

We rejoice to see her.

And finally when all the leaves are fallen
and the earth is covered with snow,
we come back and are cosy in our old home—
for winter is here again."

"What nonsense!" screamed the chickens,
  the ducks, the peacock, and the geese;
  for they had understood nothing of all this.

"Do you call that happiness?"

And the barnyard fowl who preferred
to go on preening, stuffing themselves,
and quarrelling, turned their backs on the owls
and went on living as before.

But the owls snuggled still closer
to one another,
blinked their big round eyes,
and went on thinking
their wise thoughts.